Samuel French Acting Edition

I0589022

Through the Yellow Hour

by Adam Rapp

SAMUELFRENCH.COM   SAMUELFRENCH.CO.UK

FOR PRODUCTION ENQUIRIES

UNITED STATES AND CANADA
Info@SamuelFrench.com
1-866-598-8449

UNITED KINGDOM AND EUROPE
Plays@SamuelFrench.co.uk
020-7255-4302

Each title is subject to availability from Samuel French, depending upon country of performance. Please be aware that *THROUGH THE YELLOW HOUR* may not be licensed by Samuel French in your territory. Professional and amateur producers should contact the nearest Samuel French office or licensing partner to verify availability.

MUSIC USE NOTE

Licensees are solely responsible for obtaining formal written permission from copyright owners to use copyrighted music in the performance of this play and are strongly cautioned to do so. If no such permission is obtained by the licensee, then the licensee must use only original music that the licensee owns and controls. Licensees are solely responsible and liable for all music clearances and shall indemnify the copyright owners of the play(s) and their licensing agent, Samuel French, against any costs, expenses, losses and liabilities arising from the use of music by licensees. Please contact the appropriate music licensing authority in your territory for the rights to any incidental music.

IMPORTANT BILLING AND CREDIT REQUIREMENTS

If you have obtained performance rights to this title, please refer to your licensing agreement for important billing and credit requirements.

THROUGH THE YELLOW HOUR premiered at Rattlestick Playwrights Theater in New York City on September 13, 2012. The performance was directed by Adam Rapp, with set design by Andromache Chalfant, lighting design by Keith Parham, costume design by Jessica Pabst, and sound design by Christina Frederickson. The cast was as follows:

ELLEN	Hani Furstenberg
MAUDE	Danielle Slavick
HAKIM	Alok Tewari
DEAD MAN	Brian Mendes
DOCTOR	Matt Pilieci
CLAIRE	Joanne Tucker
DARIUS	Vladimir Versailles

CHARACTERS

ELLEN

MAUDE

HAKIM

MAN/DEAD MAN

DOCTOR

CLAIRE

DARIUS

I.

(A railroad apartment in the East Village.)

(A typhoid wall with the glass blown out, a few shards remaining, separates the upstage and downstage areas. In the middle of the downstage area, a bathtub raised on a small platform. Up right, a toilet, also raised, a shower curtain ringing it. A few items of laundry are hanging to dry on the circular shower curtain dowel; off of this, a makeshift laundry line extending to the stage-left wall, laundry hanging off this as well. Down right, an old iron front door with a peephole and a standard bolt lock. Both sides of the door have been tagged with graffiti. Down left, a dead fireplace. Just downstage of it is a taped-out two-foot-by-two-foot box on the floor, completed with grey duct tape. In the corner, a hurricane oil lamp, a flashlight, a box of matches, a small space heater. Very few items of furniture, if any. There is a skylight over the bathtub, newspaper duct-taped to the glass.)

(The ceiling of the downstage area is collapsing. We see conduit, cracked beams, rotted lath.)

(Upstage of the typhoid wall is a locked cupboard secured with a steel, U-shaped bike lock, a non-working sink. Stage right of this arrangement are a few nests of bedding: sleeping bags, blankets, pillows, twisted sheets, unseen.)

(Two street-facing windows are covered with old newspaper and duct tape. The stage-left window is secured with a gate. The top half of the stage-right window has been blasted out and is dressed with a dark blanket. There is a bureau under this window.)

(It is daytime. Natural light comes in through the rifts in the ceiling, glows behind the newspapered windows in the area upstage of the typhoid wall.)

(Sweltering heat.)

*(**ELLEN** is sleeping on the floor in front of the fireplace, facing upstage. At a glance, it appears that she might be dead. On the mantle of the fireplace, a handgun.)*

(The sound of distant bombs, artillery fire from the street, a fighter jet passing overhead.)

*(The shadow of a figure passes across the upstage-left window, then the right. We see his shadow somehow hoist itself up and ease into the poorly occluded, blasted-out window. He enters through the dark blanket. His feet find purchase on the bureau. He manages to defy physics, entering quietly. He quietly lowers himself off the bureau. He is large, with long, ash-covered, unwieldy hair. He wears a gas mask and a long, dark overcoat, which is caked in ash. His shoes are spoiled and worn through the soles, wrapped in duct tape. He quietly crosses through the upstage area toward the sink and cabinet, stops in the entryway of the typhoid wall, simply watches **ELLEN** sleeping beside the fireplace. He removes his gas mask. He is fully bearded. His face is filthy.)*

(He shouts in Portuguese.)

(ELLEN wakes with a start, confused. She stands.)

(The MAN starts to sing a song in Portuguese.)*

ELLEN. What do you want.

*(The MAN starts speaking in Portuguese. ELLEN grabs the gun off the mantle, cocks it, aims it at him. The MAN holds his hands up, vigilant. He starts to act confused. He sings a song.** He stops. He cries. In a real way. He starts rooting through his pockets. He pleads with ELLEN. He laughs, starts to sing again. He is clearly out of his mind. This confuses ELLEN, and she lowers the gun a bit. He turns upstage briefly, still laughing, and then quickly rushes her with a small crowbar.)*

*(ELLEN shoots him in the chest. He drops the crowbar, lurches toward her. She shoots him again, at very close proximity. He hurls his body onto her and they grapple. He starts to laugh and sing.*** The grapple turns into a strange dance. After a few revolutions, ELLEN manages to push him into the corner just upstage of the fireplace. He slides down the wall, which is covered in his own exit-wound blood. He is still holding ELLEN. He is still laughing, out of his mind.)*

(ELLEN manages to free herself, still holding the gun. Her face and torso are covered in blood.)

(Blackout.)

(Lights up.)

(An hour later.)

(**ELLEN** *stands over the bathtub, uses dishwashing detergent to scrub blood out of the shirt she was wearing when the man broke in. She is wearing another shirt, an old tank top. Her face, her arms, her neck and chest are clean. We now see that she wears a makeshift necklace containing a key. The water runs as she scrubs the shirt clean with a heightened intensity.*)

(*In the corner, just upstage of the fireplace, the* **MAN** *sits, his legs outstretched. His body trembles. He is still alive, but barely.*)

(**ELLEN** *has blocked the upstage-right window with a large piece of scavenged plywood.*)

(*In the bathtub, she scrubs her shirt.*)

(*A knock on the door.*)

(*She stops the water, drops the shirt.*)

ELLEN. Who's there.

VOICE. *(Offstage.)* Maude.

ELLEN. Maude who?

MAUDE. *(Offstage.)* Just Maude.

ELLEN. Am I supposed to know you?

MAUDE. *(Offstage.)* China sent me.

ELLEN. China the Country?

MAUDE. *(Offstage.)* China from Third Street.

ELLEN. I need more than that.

MAUDE. *(Offstage.)* Funnyface China with the bad leg.

ELLEN. She sent you for what?

MAUDE. *(Offstage.)* What do you think?

ELLEN. What do I fucking *think*?

MAUDE. *(Offstage.)* I have what you need.

ELLEN. I need a lot of things.

MAUDE. *(Offstage.)* Yeah, you and me both.

ELLEN. Are you alone?

MAUDE. *(Offstage.)* Sort of, yes.

> *(The* **MAN** *continues trembling in the corner.)*

ELLEN. Is what you have bigger than a breadbox?

MAUDE. *(Offstage.)* It still might actually fit *inside* a breadbox.

ELLEN. How much does it weigh?

MAUDE. *(Offstage.)* Eight pounds, seven ounces.

> *(***ELLEN*** grabs the gun, which had been set at her feet.)*

I think there's a wild dog out here.

ELLEN. *(Stopping.)* It's not a dog, it's a boy.

> *(The* **MAN** *in the corner expels white material from his mouth, dies.)*

MAUDE. *(Offstage.)* Jesus. He sounds like an animal.

> *(The sound of the boy from the hallway.)*

(Offstage.) Can you hear that?

ELLEN. Don't touch him, he's septic. He has abscesses.

MAUDE. *(Offstage.)* Please...

> *(***ELLEN*** approaches the door, looks through the peephole, opens the door. The hallway is dark.)*

> *(***MAUDE*** stands in the entrance, wearing a blue bonnet on her head, as well as a gas mask, a large backpack worn in the front, boots. She also wears a dress over jeans. She is covered with what appears to be ash, a white, filmy soot.)*

> *(The sound of the sick boy is almost overwhelming.)*

ELLEN. Stay there.

> *(She steps into the hall, unseen.)*

> *(A gunshot.)*

> *(The sound of the suffering boy ceases.)*

(**MAUDE** *remains in the doorway.*)

ELLEN. *(Still in the hallway.)* Get in.

(**MAUDE** *enters the apartment.* **ELLEN** *follows her in, closes the door behind her, bolts it shut.*)

Go stand in the box.

(**MAUDE** *crosses toward the fireplace, stands inside the taped-out box.*)

Take your bonnet off.

(**MAUDE** *does so.*)

Your mask too.

(**MAUDE** *does so. She is white, American, youthful, dirty.*)

Do you have any weapons?

(**MAUDE** *reaches into a pocket of her backpack, produces a small, retractable knife. She undoes it, shows the blade, returns it to its safe position.*)

Slide it over.

(**MAUDE** *does so.* **ELLEN** *retrieves it, puts it in her pocket.*)

I'll give it back when you leave.

MAUDE. Was that boy from the building?

ELLEN. He wandered in off the street.

MAUDE. How long had he been there?

ELLEN. A few days.

MAUDE. It's a miracle he made it up here. That stairwell's blown to shit.

ELLEN. You obviously managed the ladder. Let's see it.

(**MAUDE** *opens the backpack, reaches into it, removes an infant secured in cardboard, its face covered with an infant's gas mask.*)

Female?

MAUDE. Of course.

>（**ELLEN** *takes the infant to the area upstage of the typhoid wall.*)

ELLEN. *(Turning back.)* Don't leave the box.

>*(She places the infant in an unseen sterilized incubator bin. She removes the cardboard and the small gas mask. The infant cries.* **ELLEN** *produces a pediatric ear thermometer, takes the infant's temperature.)*

MAUDE. She's in perfect health.

ELLEN. It'd certainly be in your best interest.

MAUDE. Fever?

ELLEN. *(Entering the downstage area.)* Take off your dress.

MAUDE. Why?

ELLEN. Because I want to see if you're infected.

MAUDE. I'm not.

ELLEN. Take off your fucking dress.

>*(Still in the box,* **MAUDE** *removes her dress. She wears no bra. She is filthy dirty. There is a growth of hair under her arms.)*

Turn around.

>*(***MAUDE** *turns a circle.)*

Slow down.

>*(***MAUDE** *does so, completes the circle.)*

Everything.

>*(***MAUDE** *removes her boots, her jeans, her underwear, her socks.* **ELLEN** *gestures for her to turn another circle. She does so.* **ELLEN** *points to the back of her leg.)*

What's that?

MAUDE. A bruise.

ELLEN. From what?

MAUDE. I probably bumped into something. It's not exactly Swan Lake out there...

> *(Lowering herself carefully to retrieve something from her backpack.)*

I have diapers.

> *(**ELLEN** nods. **MAUDE** tosses her a bundle of three or four cloth diapers.)*

I have tampons, too. You want some?

ELLEN. Sure.

> *(**MAUDE** tosses her a ziplock bag containing tampons.)*

Stay there.

> *(She crosses upstage of the typhoid wall with the diapers and tampons, puts them away, examines the baby.)*

Has she been fed?

MAUDE. Just now. Changed her diaper before we set out.

ELLEN. Set out from where?

MAUDE. Delancey Street.

ELLEN. Delancey and what?

MAUDE. Willett. There was a small group of us hiding in a tunnel under the Williamsburg Bridge. Or what's left of it anyway.

ELLEN. How many were you?

MAUDE. There were four of us. But we had to get out. We all went our separate ways this morning. Can I put my clothes back on?

> *(**ELLEN** nods. **MAUDE** dresses.)*

That's some door.

ELLEN. Definitely a door you can trust.

MAUDE. You'd probably have a better chance busting through the wall...

What's up with that window?

ELLEN. It's a work in progress.

(**MAUDE** *points to a rectangular vented unit over the cupboard.*)

MAUDE. What's that thing?

ELLEN. Air cleaner.

MAUDE. Where'd you get it?

ELLEN. Traded for it.

MAUDE. What'd you have to give up?

ELLEN. A round-trip vacation to Tahiti.

MAUDE. Seriously.

ELLEN. My recently reclaimed virginity.

MAUDE. Is that even possible?

ELLEN. At times of chaos you can reclaim just about anything, right?

MAUDE. You have electricity?

(**ELLEN** *enters with a milk crate, starts taking down her dry laundry.*)

ELLEN. There's a group of Egg Heads occupying a building down the block.

They figured out how to turn the electricity on, so there's juice between First and A, from here to Seventh Street. I figure if I keep the lights off, maintain a low profile, they won't bother.

MAUDE. Rats?

ELLEN. None yet today.

(*She crosses upstage of the typhoid wall with her dry laundry, starts to put it away.*)

MAUDE. You got any clean water?

ELLEN. Yes.

MAUDE. Can I have some?

(**ELLEN** *crosses to a kettle, pours water into a bowl, hands the bowl to* **MAUDE**. **MAUDE** *drinks it voraciously, finishes, hands the bowl back.* **ELLEN** *crosses upstage of it, places it in the sink.*)

MAUDE. You forget how good it tastes... That burner works, huh?

>   (**ELLEN** *nods.*)

Toilet?

ELLEN. It flushes.

MAUDE. Who'd you have to fuck for these digs?

ELLEN. My husband. It was our home.

MAUDE. Where is he?

ELLEN. He disappeared a week after the worst of the bombing stopped. Went out to get food, never came back.

MAUDE. How long has it been?

ELLEN. Fifty-two days.

MAUDE. What was his name?

ELLEN. Why?

MAUDE. You run into people.

ELLEN. His name is utterly forgettable.

MAUDE. When the shit hits the fan you'd be surprised at what your memory is capable of.

ELLEN. Paul.

MAUDE. What did he look like?

ELLEN. Six-one. Medium build. Long brown hair. He was growing a beard. Blue Eyes. Scar under his lower lip.

MAUDE. Kids?

ELLEN. No.

MAUDE. Were things good between you?

ELLEN. Yes, why.

MAUDE. It's not uncommon for people to use times like this as a means.

ELLEN. A means to what.

MAUDE. Flee.

ELLEN. He wasn't fleeing. He was going out for food.

>   (*She crosses to the door, looks out the peephole.*)

MAUDE. What happened to all your stuff?

ELLEN. I traded most of it away. There was a guy who used to come by with nine-volt batteries, iodine pills.

MAUDE. What'd you have to give up for the gun?

ELLEN. A case of canned sardines, a DVD of *Last Tango in Paris*, our flat-screen TV, my engagement ring and some tasteless sexual acts.

MAUDE. You mention sardines and my stomach moans like some lost mammal in a cave. What I would kill for a tin of sardines.

> (**ELLEN** *crosses to the cupboard, removes a can of peaches, opens the top.* **MAUDE** *steps toward the peaches.*)

Peaches.

ELLEN. Back to the box.

> (**MAUDE** *takes the peaches back to the box, eats them ravenously, gulps the syrup.* **ELLEN** *takes the peaches away before* **MAUDE** *can finish them, crosses upstage with them, sets them near the sink.*)
>
> (*The baby cries.* **ELLEN** *moves to her.*)
>
> (**MAUDE** *points to the skylight.*)

MAUDE. Don't you worry about them coming in from the roof?

ELLEN. It's a clusterfuck of razor wire and broken glass up there. Besides, this building means nothing to them. It's in the middle of the block.

MAUDE. Eventually they'll take it.

ELLEN. Eventually the sun will explode and we'll all turn into elegant intergalactic sludge.

> (**MAUDE** *points to the* **DEAD MAN** *on the floor.*)

MAUDE. What happened to him?

ELLEN. He had a bad day.

MAUDE. You knew him?

ELLEN. He broke in. Came at me with a crowbar and I shot him. The shame is he still had his balls. If I would've known that I would've made him jerk off into a Dixie cup, and then killed him.

MAUDE. Maybe he was from Belleview? I heard how the last wave of male patients weren't castrated.

ELLEN. I suppose the Egg Heads theorize the crazies' psycho sperm will weaken the gene pool.

MAUDE. You're just gonna leave him there?

ELLEN. He adds texture to the room.

MAUDE. What happened to the crowbar?

ELLEN. I swallowed it.

> *(Beat.)*

MAUDE. So do I sleep in the box too?

ELLEN. Come here.

> (**MAUDE** *crosses upstage of the typhoid wall,*
> *looks toward the sleeping area.)*

It's not the Hyatt but it's more comfortable than it looks.

MAUDE. China from Third Street said I get three days.

ELLEN. Two.

MAUDE. She said three.

ELLEN. China from Third Street's a deluded menopausal part-time heroin addict and she's been known to be frequently full of shit.

MAUDE. I need three.

ELLEN. And I need a fucking root canal and a bikini wax. Two is all I can do.

MAUDE. You have no idea what I've been through.

ELLEN. If you don't like it you can take her and leave.

> *(The baby cries.* **MAUDE** *doesn't move.* **ELLEN**
> *moves to the baby, stares down at her in the*
> *incubator bin.)*

MAUDE. *(Referring to the infant.)* What are you going to do with her? ...You gonna farm her?

ELLEN. Do I look like a fucking farmer?

> *(The baby makes a sound.)*

MAUDE. She's got a twin sister.

ELLEN. And?

MAUDE. Cut me in on whatever you got going and I'll go get her.

ELLEN. Who said I needed another one?

> (**MAUDE** *crosses down to her backpack, puts her gas mask away, clearly frustrated.*)

I'm sorry.

> (**MAUDE** *doesn't respond.*)

So what happens in three days?

MAUDE. I'm getting out of here.

ELLEN. How?

MAUDE. There's a hidden undertunnel below the D train. A group of us are making a run for it. An armored bus is picking us up in Van Cortlandt Park.

ELLEN. And then what?

MAUDE. New Hampshire, Vermont, hopefully Canada.

ELLEN. Risky.

MAUDE. No riskier than staying here.

> (*She puts her hair up with an elastic band.*)

ELLEN. (*Referring to her neck.*) Looks like you've already been accounted for.

MAUDE. It's fake. I'm not on the database.

ELLEN. Where you get the bonnet?

MAUDE. I have my ways.

> (**ELLEN** *retrieves the bonnet, reads something on the inside.*)

The number matches.

ELLEN. You killed somebody for this.

> (**MAUDE** *says nothing.* **ELLEN** *crosses to the toilet, sits high on the tank, her feet on the toilet seat.*)

MAUDE. What's your name?

ELLEN. Really?

MAUDE. Yeah, really. China wouldn't tell me.

ELLEN. Dave.

MAUDE. Come on. You know mine.

ELLEN. Not on your life. Besides, I could tell you anything. You say you're Maude but you could just as likely be Brenda. Or Betty.

MAUDE. I'm fucking Maude. Maude Elizabeth Miller from Kankakee, Illinois.

ELLEN. So I'll call you fucking Maude Elizabeth Miller from Kankakee, Illinois and you can call me whatever you want.

MAUDE. You look like a Caitlin.

ELLEN. I'm not.

MAUDE. A Caitlin or a Ginny.

ELLEN. You're saying I look like a parochial school eighth-grader in a tartan skirt?

MAUDE. You're clean as shit.

ELLEN. You should've seen me an hour ago.

(*Reports of automatic weapons from the street.*)

Who the fuck could they possibly be firing at? They get off on shooting deli bags stuck in trees.

MAUDE. What trees?

ELLEN. Deli bags stuck in lampposts.

MAUDE. What lampposts?

ELLEN. Deli bags floating in mysterious penumbral ash. I've seen lampposts.

MAUDE. Two months ago maybe.

ELLEN. There's a lamppost on my corner.

MAUDE. When was the last time you went outside? We're approaching a state of rubble. It's starting to look like Chicago out there. Gaza. Seriously how long has it been?

ELLEN. Going on two months.

MAUDE. And you're surviving on peaches?

ELLEN. Pretty much.

> *(Beat.)*

MAUDE. Would you mind if I took a bath?

ELLEN. Help yourself.

> (**MAUDE** *crosses to the bathtub.*)

MAUDE. Water's okay?

ELLEN. It's a little rusty. Just don't drink it.

> (**MAUDE** *plugs the drain, starts the bath, holds her hand under the nozzle.*)

MAUDE. Hot water. Are you serious?

> *(The tub fills.)*

> (**MAUDE** *removes her clothes, gets in the tub.* **ELLEN** *gives her a bar of soap.*)

Thanks.

> *(She washes over the following.)*

So don't you get lonely being here all by yourself?

ELLEN. Sometimes.

MAUDE. What do you do to pass the time?

ELLEN. Flatten cans. Rearrange my newspaper collection. Talk to the sandbags.

MAUDE. What do the sandbags tell you?

ELLEN. The Dow is up four points. Tangelos are all the rage. Mike and the Mechanics are making a comeback.

> *(She grabs a tea kettle, fills it with water from the bathtub.)*

MAUDE. They say there's going to be an election.

ELLEN. When?

MAUDE. In a matter of weeks. As soon as the Egg Heads stabilize Midtown. As of Wednesday, if you're a woman on the street caught not wearing a blue bonnet you'll be hanged in Union Square... Why aren't you trying to get to Pennsylvania?

ELLEN. What's in Pennsylvania?

MAUDE. There are barges you can get on. They're traveling south along the shallows of Lake Erie. But first you have to get to Buffalo.

ELLEN. Go all the way up to Buffalo to get on a barge?

MAUDE. If you make it to Pennsylvania there are groups helping people get to Youngstown, Ohio. Apparently Youngstown, Ohio is still safe.

ELLEN. I guess I have a pretty good reason for sticking around.

MAUDE. You think he's still alive? You know what they're doing to all the men, right?

ELLEN. You can survive a castration.

MAUDE. If done properly, but who said they're following rules? They started out removing the testicles, but it's become much more savage. It's now a joyous, defiant act of celebration. I've seen shriveled penises arranged on necklaces.

ELLEN. I have dreams that he's pounding on the door.

(**MAUDE** *dunks her hair, soaps it.*)

MAUDE. What did your husband do?

ELLEN. He taught high school.

MAUDE. What subject?

ELLEN. Why?

MAUDE. Because I'm curious.

ELLEN. You crave the details?

MAUDE. I'm just trying to make conversation.

ELLEN. (*Getting* **MAUDE** *a towel.*) When one's trying to make conversation one talks about the weather, the price of cigarettes.

MAUDE. Speaking of cigarettes, if you know a little Arabic or Chinese you can score a pack of Camel Lights for a case of Coke Classic...

ELLEN. What about Spanish?

MAUDE. Spanish'll get you a can of corn. The Egg Heads don't touch alcohol but they fucking smoke like a herd of blue-blooded capitalists.

(She stops the water.)

ELLEN. Paul taught sophomore English at Humanities High School. At night and on weekends he wrote short stories about deer hunting and teenagers railing against middle-class cul-de-sac culture and growing up Catholic. He was starting to take notes on a novel about a young Indiana boy who decides to walk to the Arctic Circle. He was never published. He has large wide hands and when he sweats his skin smells like cinnamon.

> *(The baby cries.* **ELLEN** *crosses to her, watches her.)*
>
> *(***MAUDE*** *gets out of the tub, dries herself, dresses.)*

She has your eyes... Who's the father?

MAUDE. He left.

ELLEN. When?

MAUDE. First night of the bombing. Snuck out just before dawn. He thought I was sleeping. He cleaned out the fridge, took our block of kitchen knives, a backpack of clothes, all our Hefty bags and went down the fire escape. Didn't even kiss his little girls goodbye. Didn't even bother to close the window... Should I leave the water?

> *(***ELLEN*** *unstops the drain.)*

ELLEN. Why didn't you stop him?

MAUDE. I don't know. I guess because things had dissolved between us.

ELLEN. How long had you been together?

MAUDE. Five years.

ELLEN. Had you ever loved him?

MAUDE. Early on.

ELLEN. What did he do?

MAUDE. He was a social worker. We lived off his trust fund.

ELLEN. Where?

MAUDE. Fort Greene.

ELLEN. *(Sitting on the toilet seat.)* ...Wow.

MAUDE. Wow what.

ELLEN. To leave your wife and children –

MAUDE. We weren't married. He fucked around on me pretty much nonstop.

It got to the point where I couldn't stand the sight of him.

ELLEN. But regardless of how you felt about each other, he abandoned his daughters.

MAUDE. As am I.

ELLEN. You're giving her a better life.

MAUDE. I don't know that.

ELLEN. She's going to have a better life, trust me.

MAUDE. China said you were a Nurse.

ELLEN. I like to think I still am.

MAUDE. What kind?

ELLEN. Pediatrics.

MAUDE. That must have been intense.

ELLEN. You want to learn about courage, spend some time with sick children.

Adults tend to get petty when they're dying. Children are all grace.

MAUDE. Where did you work?

ELLEN. New York Presbyterian.

(*Beat.*)

MAUDE. China also told me you have drugs.

ELLEN. China would know.

MAUDE. What kind?

ELLEN. You're not sick.

MAUDE. I'm not asking because I'm sick.

ELLEN. Morphine. Demerol. Dilaudid. Vicodin. Percocet.

MAUDE. Can I have some Dilaudid?

ELLEN. She opts for luxury.

MAUDE. I'll get you off.

ELLEN. Not sure I'd be into that.

MAUDE. Never been with a woman?

> (**ELLEN** *doesn't answer.*)

I'm good.

> (**ELLEN** *says nothing.*)

I'd settle for two Vicodins. I'll make you cum so hard you'll forget about the heat.

ELLEN. When'd you start using?

MAUDE. Maybe a month ago. I've mostly been feeding her formula, so...

ELLEN. Where's the formula?

> (**MAUDE** *grabs the backpack, produces a large jug of concentrated formula.*)

You've *mostly* been feeding her formula?

MAUDE. Mostly, yeah.

ELLEN. Are you still lactating?

> (**MAUDE** *nods.*)

When was your last fix?

MAUDE. About a week ago.

ELLEN. How's her appetite been?

MAUDE. Moderate.

ELLEN. Feed her. Then I'll give you a shot.

MAUDE. Dilaudid?

ELLEN. Demerol.

MAUDE. She's not hungry.

ELLEN. Feed her.

> (**MAUDE** *crosses to the infant, removes her from the incubator bin, bears her breast, feeds her while leaning against the bureau.* **ELLEN** *looks on from the doorway in the typhoid wall.*)

What does it feel like?

MAUDE. Like something's gently tugging at your soul.

ELLEN. Is that good or bad?

MAUDE. I guess it depends.

ELLEN. On what?

MAUDE. The condition of your soul.

ELLEN. What's her name?

MAUDE. Whatever you want it to be.

> (**ELLEN** crosses downstage of the typhoid wall, giving **MAUDE** privacy. She stands downstage of the fireplace. **MAUDE** quietly sings a song,* more for herself than her child. Something in the song troubles her and she stops. **ELLEN** turns back. They look at each other. **ELLEN** turns away.)
>
> (Eventually **MAUDE** holds the baby, connecting with her, bringing her head to the crook of her neck, gentle with her. She places the baby back in the incubator bin, crosses to the entryway of the typhoid wall, waiting.)

ELLEN. Can you come out here, please?

> (**MAUDE** does so, sits on the toilet.)
>
> (**ELLEN** unlocks the bike lock cupboard with the key around her neck, opens the cupboard, removes a vial, a hypodermic needle, an alcohol wipe. She relocks the cupboard, crosses to **MAUDE** on the toilet, starts to clean her arm with an alcohol wipe.)
>
> (**MAUDE** kisses **ELLEN**. **ELLEN** doesn't resist. **MAUDE** grabs at **ELLEN**'s breast, her crotch. It gets intense for a moment. **ELLEN** relents, gives over to the pleasure.)

---

*A license to produce *Through the Yellow Hour* does not include a performance license for any third-party or copyrighted music. Licensees should create an original composition or use music in the public domain. For further information, please see Music Use Note on page 3.

MAUDE. You sure I can't have some Dilaudid?

> (**ELLEN** *breaks from the advance.*)
>
> (*There is a momentary standoff, and then* **MAUDE** *returns to the toilet seat.* **ELLEN** *resumes cleaning* **MAUDE***'s arm, all business now, prepares the hypo.*)

Do you use it?

ELLEN. When I can't sleep sometimes I'll take a Vicodin.

MAUDE. You have yourself a regular candy store.

> (*They lock eyes for a moment, a warning from* **ELLEN**, *then* **ELLEN** *continues.*)

Can I do it?

> (**ELLEN** *hands her the needle, stands there.* **MAUDE** *looks at her as if to ask for privacy.* **ELLEN** *crosses into the other room, upstage of the typhoid wall.* **MAUDE** *shoots up, using a black shoelace worn around her wrist.*)

ELLEN. If you're going to be sick please use the toilet.

> (**MAUDE** *waits for the shot to kick in.*)

MAUDE. During the Yellow Hour sometimes I go to the East River and just watch the sun coming up... The sickly water going surprisingly silver...the rare seagull... So still in its flight it looks somehow pinned to the sky... It's amazing to me that there are still seagulls...

ELLEN. That's when Paul went out looking for food – during the supposed Yellow Hour. So much for the promised six a.m. armistice.

> (**MAUDE** *slides off the toilet seat, settles on the floor.*)

MAUDE. For some reason the Egg Heads really do leave you alone at the water.

It must be a religious thing.

ELLEN. Maybe they're afraid Allah will appear on a jet ski.

MAUDE. Now there's an image.

ELLEN. I see Omar Sharif wrapped in cheesecloth.

MAUDE. I see him more like the late Ben Kingsley.

ELLEN. Sir Ben Kingsley.

MAUDE. Sir Ben Kingsley.

ELLEN. With a perfect Arabic accent.

MAUDE. And soft, dilated pupils.

> (**ELLEN** *enters the room, starts to clean up after* **MAUDE**, *taking the hypo, the vial, etc.*)

ELLEN. Or Castro. Not sure why.

MAUDE. Allah as a communist, now that's complicated.

ELLEN. Not entirely.

MAUDE. With or without the cigar?

ELLEN. Definitely without. He'd judge them accordingly, and turn them all into pork.

> (*She tidies things, then watches the infant.*)

She's quiet.

MAUDE. Thank God for that.

ELLEN. Where did you have her?

MAUDE. At home. While squatting over a birthing pool of warm salt water.

ELLEN. Was it painful?

MAUDE. It was the worst thing I've ever felt in my life. When it was finally over I looked down and saw these two creatures swimming in place. Like a pair of skinned otters. Screeching. Terrified.

> (*After* **MAUDE** *has nodded off,* **ELLEN** *crosses to the infant, lifts her out of the incubator bin, holds her close, paces a bit, stops in the entrance of the typhoid wall, bears her breast, brings the infant to it.*)
>
> (*The* **DEAD MAN** *opens his eyes, stares at* **ELLEN**. *They lock eyes.*)
>
> (*Blackout.*)

II.

(Middle of the night.)

*(**MAUDE** and **ELLEN** are asleep in the nests, upstage of the typhoid wall.)*

*(The **DEAD MAN** is still in the corner.)*

*(A Middle-Eastern **MAN** enters with a key. He's suffered severe lacerations to his neck and arms. On his head, he wears a filthy turban. He wears a thick beard, many weeks old. His eyes are damaged and he is almost blind. In his left arm he holds a white, egg-shaped helmet. Mask. He wears military-style clothes. They are filthy, stained, bloody. He has great difficulty walking, occasionally clutches at his left side in a protective manner. The door closes.)*

*(**ELLEN** enters from upstage, training a flashlight on his face, as well as the gun.)*

ELLEN. Don't move. I have a gun.

*(The **MAN** awkwardly shuffles a bit.)*

One more step and I'll blow your fucking head off.

MAN. I'm not moving.

ELLEN. Lock the door.

MAN. I can't.

ELLEN. Why?

MAN. Because you will kill me.

ELLEN. You can move to lock the door.

*(The **MAN** turns, feels the door, figures out the bolt, locks it, slowly turns back.)*

Put your hands over your head.

(He puts his right hand over his head, still holding the helmet with his left hand.)

Who are you?

MAN. Hakim.

ELLEN. Hakim who?

HAKIM. Ibraheem.

ELLEN. Hakim Ibraheem?

HAKIM. Yes, Hakim Ibraheem. I'm not an intruder, I assure you.

ELLEN. I'd say by most standard definitions you more than qualify.

HAKIM. Are you Ellen?

ELLEN. Stop fucking moving!

HAKIM. Sorry. I am very nervous.

ELLEN. Why do you have a key to this apartment?

HAKIM. Are you not Ellen?

ELLEN. Answer the fucking question.

HAKIM. Because I knew your husband.

ELLEN. You knew Paul?

HAKIM. Yes.

ELLEN. How?

HAKIM. I was with him.

ELLEN. Where?

HAKIM. In a building. On Orchard Street.

ELLEN. With him for how long?

HAKIM. For several weeks.

ELLEN. What building on Orchard Street?

HAKIM. It was just a building.

(Wincing in pain.)

An apartment building.

ELLEN. Doing what?

HAKIM. We were prisoners.

ELLEN. Why Orchard Street?

HAKIM. I do not know the reason. This is where they took us.

ELLEN. Who?

HAKIM. The Egg Heads.

ELLEN. Paul gave you the key to this apartment?

HAKIM. Yes.

ELLEN. Why?

HAKIM. May I move? I have to get something out of my pocket.

ELLEN. What.

HAKIM. A letter.

ELLEN. Why are you holding one of those fucking helmets?

HAKIM. Because I took it from my captor. It is the only way I would have made it through the streets… May I give you the letter?

ELLEN. Fine.

> (**HAKIM** *slowly goes into his pocket, produces a piece of torn cloth.*)

HAKIM. It is from Paul. Please take it.

> (*He hands* **ELLEN** *a piece of folded cloth. He is shaking, very weak, afraid.*)

> (**ELLEN** *crosses to the fireplace, unfolds the cloth, reads it.*)

ELLEN. Is he still alive?

> (**HAKIM** *says nothing.*)

Just tell me.

HAKIM. I was with him when he died. I held him in my arms.

> (**ELLEN** *drops the piece of cloth, rushes to the toilet, lifts the lid, vomits.*)

I am sorry for your loss.

> (**ELLEN** *vomits again.*)

> (*Sounds from the street. The sound of the baby.*)

What is that? Is that a child?

> (**MAUDE** *is awake now.*)

ELLEN. Yes.

HAKIM. Who does it belong to?

ELLEN. It doesn't belong to anyone. I'm just taking care of it.

HAKIM. It is so young.

(The baby cries as **MAUDE** *cares for it. Eventually the crying ceases.)*

ELLEN. Was Paul tortured?

HAKIM. We all were, yes.

ELLEN. How many of you were there?

HAKIM. There were twelve of us.

ELLEN. How many of you survived?

HAKIM. Only three.

ELLEN. Were you a prisoner too?

HAKIM. Yes, but at first I had privileges.

ELLEN. Why?

HAKIM. Because I know Arabic.

(Wincing in pain.)

I was their translator.

ELLEN. Privileges meaning what?

HAKIM. Meaning they would spare me certain abuses.

ELLEN. Would they feed you?

HAKIM. Very little.

ELLEN. Would they feed the others?

HAKIM. Yes, but nothing edible.

ELLEN. Like what?

HAKIM. Feces. The stomach from a dog. Insects. Things like this.

*(***ELLEN*** stands quickly.)*

ELLEN. Where are you from?

HAKIM. Iraq.

ELLEN. Why were you captured?

HAKIM. I was a visiting professor at Fordham University. I dressed like an American.

ELLEN. You're not dressed like an American now.

HAKIM. Like I said, these were taken from one of my captors.

ELLEN. What part of Iraq are you from?

HAKIM. My family is from Mosul. It's in the north. On the Tigris River.

ELLEN. Are you Muslim?

HAKIM. I was raised Christian.

ELLEN. Bullshit.

HAKIM. I truly was. There are many Christians in Mosul.

ELLEN. What, like Iraqi Lutherans?

HAKIM. There are Lutherans, yes. But I was raised Roman Catholic.

ELLEN. I don't believe you.

HAKIM. Our Father who art in heaven hallowed be thy name thy kingdom come thy will be done on earth as it is in heaven give us this day our daily bread and forgive us our trespasses –

ELLEN. Okay, okay, okay.

HAKIM. I can also recite this in Arabic.

ELLEN. What were you teaching at Fordham?

HAKIM. Computer Science.

ELLEN. What's wrong with your eyes?

HAKIM. I cannot see so good.

ELLEN. Are you blind?

HAKIM. In one of them, yes.

    (Wincing in pain.)

In the other I can still make out shapes.

ELLEN. How did that happen?

HAKIM. I do not remember exactly. All I know is that I was struck with something very cold and sharp and then my eye emptied out and I could no longer see.

ELLEN. What happened to your privileges?

HAKIM. I was often sick and I lost my purpose.

ELLEN. You were often sick? Are you infected?

HAKIM. *No!* What I mean to say is that I did not have the stomach for their methods. They saw me pitying the others. So they turned on me.

(*The sound of a fighter jet passing overhead.*)

ELLEN. How did you escape?

HAKIM. Three of us overtook the guard when he fell asleep. We broke his neck and confiscated his weapon and killed the others, who were in the kitchen, preparing a meal.

ELLEN. Was Paul part of that three?

HAKIM. No.

ELLEN. When did he die?

HAKIM. Approximately five days ago. But I could not possibly tell you precisely.

ELLEN. Why not?

HAKIM. Because the room was quite dark. Time lost its shape.

(*Beat.*)

ELLEN. Was Paul tortured badly?

HAKIM. Very badly, yes.

ELLEN. What did they do to him?

HAKIM. I should not tell you.

ELLEN. You have to.

HAKIM. I promised him that if I ever found you I would not.

(**ELLEN** *pulls the gun on him. He senses it more than sees it.*)

Please, Ellen. I beg of you.

(*He goes to his knees, hands outstretched to her, bowing his head.*)

Please, please, please, please, please, please...

ELLEN. If you want to live tell me what they did to Paul.

HAKIM. I gave him my word –

*(**ELLEN** shoots the **DEAD MAN** in the corner. The dead body jumps. The baby starts crying. **ELLEN** continues training the flashlight and gun at **HAKIM**'s head.)*

Okay, okay, okay!

*(The baby continues crying. **MAUDE** quiets her.)*

(Still prostrated, head down.) First they beat him. For several hours. Until he lost consciousness.

ELLEN. With what.

HAKIM. With their fists. The backs of their hands. Their boots. The butts of their rifles. Bricks. The lid of a toilet seat. A broomstick. A clock radio. A sack filled with coins. He spat out several teeth.

ELLEN. And then what.

HAKIM. After he regained consciousness they broke his left femur.

ELLEN. How?

HAKIM. They used a sledgehammer.

ELLEN. *(Stomping her foot.)* Keep going!

HAKIM. Then they broke his feet and nailed his left hand to a table and removed his fingernails and poured boiling water over his wrist.

ELLEN. And then?

HAKIM. They sodomized him with the leg from a table. And then...

*(The infant cries. **ELLEN** steps toward **HAKIM**.)*

ELLEN. If you don't tell me everything I swear to your Catholic god I will kill you.

HAKIM. Then they castrated him and stuffed his testicles into his mouth and forced him to swallow. Then they removed his eyes with a spoon and cut out his tongue. He did not live for many hours after that.

ELLEN. And while all of this was going on what were you doing?

HAKIM. I could do nothing.

ELLEN. Why not?!

HAKIM. Because they were also doing many of these things to me.

(*A fighter jet passes overhead.*)

Paul told me I would be safe here.

ELLEN. Why do you have the beard?

HAKIM. They forced me to grow it. To humiliate me. They made me pray with them too... Their prayers are actually quite beautiful. The truth is that many of the Egg Heads we were exposed to were not even Muslim. It was as if they were playing a part.

ELLEN. How do you know that?

HAKIM. I could just tell. Many of them drank alcohol, ate whatever they wanted. It was as if they were wearing costumes. Like I am now.

(*He removes the turban. His scalp is severely wounded, bloody.*)

(**ELLEN** *re-reads the letter, sobs.*)

I am so very sorry, Ellen.

ELLEN. Why did they do this?

HAKIM. There is no reason.

ELLEN. They had to have a fucking reason.

HAKIM. Because they could. It is all they know.

ELLEN. You pity them.

HAKIM. I do not believe the makers of this war are even Muslim.

ELLEN. Well then who's behind it?

HAKIM. I cannot say for sure, but the Egg Heads have too many resources.
Their weapons are too advanced. Paul believed it was some corporate entity financing mercenaries. I tend to agree with him.

(Beat.)

Ellen, Paul loved you very much. He talked about you with great feeling.

ELLEN. Until they cut out his tongue.

HAKIM. He was a good man.

> (**ELLEN** *is bereft.*)

Do you have any water?

> *(She doesn't answer.)*

I am very thirsty. Please...

> (**MAUDE** *crosses to the kettle, pours him a bowl of clean water.*)

MAUDE. I have water.

> (**HAKIM** *drinks. It sounds like a dog drinking.*)

HAKIM. Thank you.

> (**ELLEN** *lowers herself to the floor, lights the hurricane lantern, turns off the flashlight.*)

ELLEN. *(To* **MAUDE**.*)* Get away from him.

MAUDE. Why?

ELLEN. Because I said so. Get the fuck away from him.

> (**MAUDE** *moves away, crosses upstage of the typhoid wall.*)
>
> (**ELLEN** *approaches* **HAKIM**, *who retreats toward the door, afraid.* **ELLEN** *sets the lantern down, takes over tending to his wounds. She tears his shirt open, uses a small light from her pocket to examine his side.*)

One of your ribs is coming through your skin.

> *(Only using the lamplight, she uses duct tape and a washcloth to cover the damaged rib.)*

HAKIM. Paul told me you had been married for five years. I am also married. My wife is in Mosul.

ELLEN. What's her name?

HAKIM. Sabeen.

ELLEN. What does she do?

HAKIM. She is a veterinarian's assistant.

ELLEN. Is she pretty?

HAKIM. I think she is very beautiful.

ELLEN. What does she look like?

HAKIM. She has long dark hair. A kind, pleasant face. Large eyes, very deep and brown.

> *(Wincing in pain.)*

Delicate, slender fingers.

ELLEN. When was the last time you saw her?

HAKIM. Many months ago.

ELLEN. Does she know you're still alive?

HAKIM. No.

ELLEN. You must miss her terribly.

HAKIM. More than I thought was humanly possible.

> *(Beat.)*

Paul told me that you and he were trying to conceive a child.

ELLEN. We'd been trying for over a year.

HAKIM. Are you with child?

ELLEN. No.

HAKIM. I am sorry. Paul would have been a good father, I am sure of this...
Sabeen and I wished to make a family, too, but that is not possible now. I am afraid I have lost feeling down there.

ELLEN. Can I see?

HAKIM. It is not so good, I assure you.

ELLEN. I might be able to help you.

> *(HAKIM tries to lower his pants.)*

May I?

> *(She helps him lower his pants. She uses the small light to examine his right leg. She pulls her hand away and it is soaked with blood.)*

HAKIM. It is bad, is it not?

ELLEN. Yes. You're still bleeding.

> *(Touching him.)* Can you feel this?

HAKIM. No.

ELLEN. This?

HAKIM. No.

ELLEN. Your femoral artery is damaged. You've lost a lot of blood. This is very serious, Hakim.

> *(She uses his turban to create a makeshift tourniquet. She pulls it tight above his wound. **HAKIM** cries out. The baby cries.)*
>
> *(Suddenly, the sound of foreign voices coming from somewhere inside the building, perhaps from the rubble below. In the other room, **MAUDE** covers the baby's mouth.)*

HAKIM. *(Afraid.)* Am I going to die?

ELLEN. *Shshshsh!*

> *(They are silent. The sound of foreign men speaking continues, somewhere below them. **ELLEN** raises the gun, waits.)*
>
> *(The voices fade.)*

HAKIM. There is no need to spare me the truth.

ELLEN. I'm going to give you something for the pain.

> *(She crosses to the cupboard. Unlocks it, produces a vial of morphine, a hypodermic needle. She closes and locks the cupboard. She starts to undo the cuff of his sleeve. **HAKIM** stops her.)*

HAKIM. Ellen, there is something else I must tell you.

> *(**ELLEN** simply looks at him.)*

HAKIM. At the end. When Paul was suffering. They forced me to take his life. It was either him or me.

ELLEN. How did you do it?

HAKIM. I cut his throat.

> (**ELLEN** *takes this in. Then:*)

ELLEN. Tell me about Mosul.

> (*She prepares the hypo, injects his arm over the following.*)

HAKIM. It is very hot there. Much hotter than here. The summers are difficult but you get used to it... We have good hospitals and a fine University. The sunsets are magnificent. There are beautiful mosques and churches...

> (*Distant thunder.*)

(*Starting to drift.*) There is a Christian monastery just south of the city called Dair Mar Elia, or St. Elijah's... It was built in the sixth century... Though it has suffered terrible damages throughout the centuries, it still stands... To this day, many Christians make great pilgrimages there... I visited it only once, when I was a child. I was struck by how small it was. It seemed as if it could only contain a few dozen men. The walls were crumbling but they still remained. It was so small to be a place of God. So inconsequential.

(*Very high now.*) I was also struck by the sounds of birds. Though I could not see them, I could hear birds. Thousands of them... I think of this place and it gives me hope for the world; that despite all the senselessness, we will remain; that the souls of people will last.

> (*The sound of rain. Water can be seen starting to leak through the ceiling. It drips on the floor.*)

> (**ELLEN** *grabs a towel and a pot from the area under the bathtub, sets it to catch the drip.*)

(With the lantern, the vial, and the hypo, **ELLEN** *crosses upstage of the typhoid wall. She sets the lantern on the floor before crossing the threshold, careful to keep the light away from the windows. She unlocks the cupboard, removes another hypodermic needle, locks the cupboard, steadies herself using the doorway in the typhoid wall, uses her key necklace to tourniquet her arm, and then injects herself with Dilaudid. She discards the empty vial and needle.)*

(She swoons for a moment, crosses downstage to the fireplace, uses the mantle to help lower herself to the floor, starts to be overtaken by the Dilaudid.)

*(***MAUDE*** enters from the upstage area, quietly crosses to* **ELLEN***, lowers herself to her knees, attempts to remove the key necklace from around* **ELLEN***'s neck.* **ELLEN** *comes to. There is a vicious, savage struggle for the necklace; choking, biting, clawing. The baby starts to cry, very loud.* **ELLEN** *manages to produce the gun, sets it to* **MAUDE***'s forehead.* **MAUDE** *quickly relents.* **ELLEN** *stands.)*

ELLEN. Get out.

(She continues training the gun on **MAUDE** *as she crosses upstage to get her backpack.)*

(The baby continues crying.)

Don't forget your knife.

(She reaches into her pocket, hands **MAUDE** *the knife, the gun still trained on her.* **MAUDE** *exits. The baby continues crying.* **ELLEN** *locks the door behind her, returns to the fireplace, again finds the floor, her back against the fireplace doors, facing* **HAKIM***.)*

(The baby continues crying.)

(It continues to rain.)

*(**ELLEN** fully gives over to the Dilaudid.)*

(Only the sound of the infant crying through the rushing rain.)

*(The **DEAD MAN** opens his eyes.)*

(The baby stops crying.)

(The rain stops.)

*(**ELLEN** and the **DEAD MAN** stare at each other. He stands and grabs the hurricane lantern. He sets it on the mantle over **ELLEN**. He reaches down and takes the piece of cloth from her, uses the lamplight to read Paul's letter.)*

DEAD MAN. Ellen.

I'm not sure if knowing matters. If truth matters. I think it does.

It is hard to write.

I have failed you.
I have failed you so many times.

I left you. I was arrogant. Naïve. I was unprepared. They caught me just after the keening. I wasn't out of the building for more than fifteen minutes.
It was easy for them. I made it easy.
False courage
stupidity.

Since Then. It has been thirty-nine days
I think.
It has been hard to count.

It is hard to find words

does not matter.

My captors
ignorant manipulated
unimportant

Players in a game

Like me.

You are stronger than me.
Smarter.
Your will does not manifest as bravado.
Your skill. Your strategy. Instinct.
You will survive.
You can. I know.

Trust. I trust you. I trust you to survive. I trust you
to find
create future
Better!
to be the
a Faith
I don't know truth.
you decide
you decide you
Make

I am sorry I ever showed you anything other than
absolute unrelenting

love and devotion.

Everything i said up until this moment seems like a lie

i have no past

i will never see you again

You are my future.

You are
are us. Me.

You. You. You.

The man who brings this letter.
Help him. If you can.

Paul.

(The **DEAD MAN** *takes the hurricane lamp, crosses to* **HAKIM**, *opens the door.* **HAKIM** *opens his eye, stands, exits. The* **DEAD MAN** *follows him out.)*

(Lights to black.)

(Lights up.)

(It is day and the **DEAD MAN** *is now upstage of the typhoid wall, holding the baby in his arms. The baby starts to cry.* **ELLEN** *looks on from the floor near the fireplace.)*

(Lights to black.)

(The baby continues crying.)

(Lights up.)

(It is evening, and the **DEAD MAN** *is now wearing his gas mask. He is facing the stage-right wall, downstage of the toilet. He uses charcoal, draws a large "X" on the wall, starts recording numbers in its four quadrants. The baby continues to cry. We also hear the* **DEAD MAN** *reciting Paul's letter backwards. The sound is everywhere.* **ELLEN** *has wedged herself into the corner, downstage of the fireplace. Her hand is on the wall. She stares at the wall, going mad.)*

(Lights to black.)

(The **DEAD MAN** *continues reciting the letter backwards.)*

(The flashlight is turned on.)

*(***ELLEN** *is lying in the taped-out box, in the fetal position, clutching the flashlight close. She is shivering, her teeth chatter. The* **DEAD MAN** *can still be heard reciting Paul's letter backwards. A cacophony of the backwards letter.)*

(Only the flashlight illuminating **ELLEN***'s shivering body, which is the only thing we see other than the faintest hint of moonlight on the upstage windows. It should almost feel as if she is floating in black space.)*

(The sound of men keening.)

(Flashlight off.)

III.

(The winter, some months later, dawn.)

(The sound of wind whistling. A cold, desolate wind. There is a feeling of calm in the street. No automatic weapons.)

(The sound of keening from the street: a wailing prayer.)

(The dead man is still on the floor, thoroughly decayed now, facing upstage, wrapped in a blanket, only his hair and skull discernible.)

(The walls have gained history.)

*(A **WOMAN** is in the apartment now, down left, near the air cleaner as well as a small space heater. Also present is a male **DOCTOR**, who is in the area upstage of the typhoid wall, examining the infant. This area has been outfitted with a very bright medical light.)*

*(The **WOMAN** is clean, white, well-dressed, very well-appointed, perhaps thirty. She is very beautiful, almost perfect in that Grace Kelly way. She is distinctly not covered in ash.)*

*(The **DOCTOR** wears a clean, white medical jumpsuit, glasses with LED spotlights, nice shoes. He also wears a long, dark beard and looks Muslim. He is very clean, no ash. He speaks well, with a high-end American accent.)*

*(Also present is a young African-American **BOY**. He wears a buttoned-down shirt, trousers, nice shoes. He sits quietly on the small step ladder, which has been set in front of the fireplace. He is very poised, very clean, no ash. His winter coat is over the back of the step ladder.)*

(ELLEN and the WOMAN speak while the DOCTOR conducts his examination of the infant.)

(ELLEN seems drawn, very tired, hungry, dehydrated. Her teeth are dim. There is yellow under her eyes. She wears layers, perhaps a thick sweater, which she hides her hands in.)

ELLEN. You've brought the snow with you.

WOMAN. Have we?

ELLEN. It hasn't snowed once this winter. You start to believe the ash is snow, but then it really snows. The difference is extraordinary.

WOMAN. Hopefully the snow will refresh the air. Thin the ash a bit.

(Pause.)

ELLEN. I wish I could offer you something.

WOMAN. We're fine, thanks.

(The keening grows in intensity for a moment.)

(Referring to the keening.) Does that happen often?

ELLEN. Every dawn. The Egg Heads park their tanks and the AK-47s cease and there's a momentary silence when you can only hear a seagull or two and then the wailing begins. I guess they figure an hour of keening affords them several more hundred tons of rubble. Big ups to Allah.

(After a brief pause.) You don't happen to have a cigarette, do you?

WOMAN. I don't smoke.

(From the upstage area, the DOCTOR produces a cigarette, crosses to ELLEN with it.)

ELLEN. Thank you.

DOCTOR. Please don't smoke that until we've gone.

WOMAN. We'd hate the child to be exposed.

(ELLEN smells the cigarette.)

ELLEN. *(To the* DOCTOR.*)* What about red wine? You got any red wine? Preferably a ten-year-old Rioja Gran Reserva with a peppery bouquet and an oaky vanilla finish? Just kidding.

WOMAN. Did you know the mother?

ELLEN. Briefly.

WOMAN. What was she like?

ELLEN. I can't really say.

WOMAN. Was she fair? Was she overweight? Did she have good skin?

ELLEN. She was fair. Thinner than most. Average skin.

WOMAN. Was she tall?

ELLEN. Taller than me.

WOMAN. Was her hair straight? Curly?

ELLEN. Her hair was dirty.

WOMAN. Go on.

ELLEN. She enjoyed long walks by the shore, sentimental coming-of-age novels, and the Beatles, post-Sergeant Pepper's. I wasn't aware that a resume was required.

WOMAN. It helps to know these things.

ELLEN. She was starting to use drugs in a pretty intense way.

WOMAN. She was an addict?

ELLEN. That was my take.

WOMAN. Narcotics?

ELLEN. Top-shelf narcotics, yes.

DOCTOR. Was she still breastfeeding?

ELLEN. Would that disqualify the infant?

WOMAN. Not necessarily.

ELLEN. She was breastfeeding intermittently.

WOMAN. Anything else?

ELLEN. She had webbed feet and a tail. And a large spotted penis protruding from her navel. That's a beautiful suit by the way.

WOMAN. Thank you.

ELLEN. Bespoke?

WOMAN. It is, as a matter of fact.

ELLEN. And your shoes. I haven't seen shoes like that in I don't know how long. Are they alligator?

WOMAN. I believe they are, yes.

ELLEN. Where did you guys fly in from, Bergdorf's?

>   *(The **WOMAN** doesn't answer.)*

Seriously, where?

>   *(Nothing.)*

Is it in the United States?

>   *(Again, nothing.)*

North America?

>   *(Yet again, nothing.)*

Well, wherever it is, is it safe there?

DOCTOR. Exponentially safer than here.

ELLEN. Why do you need an infant girl?

>   *(The **WOMAN** corrects the **BOY**'s posture. He sits up straighter.)*

WOMAN. Because at Mrs. Winship's farm there is a dearth of fertile females.

ELLEN. How could you possibly know whether or not she'll be fertile?

WOMAN. Our tests bear unequivocal results.

DOCTOR. *(From the kitchen.)* She'll be fertile. She's a bit malnourished but she'll be fertile. What have you been feeding her?

ELLEN. Peach syrup. I ran out of formula about a month ago.

WOMAN. She'll receive the best medical and nutritional care in a highly controlled environment.

ELLEN. Meaning what, she'll be kept in a locked room and forced to eat kale?

WOMAN. On the contrary. She'll be treated like royalty.

ELLEN. Lawn tennis? Croquet? Dressage? Why does she have to be white?

(The **WOMAN** *is inscrutable.)*

My contact insisted that she be white.

(Still nothing from the **WOMAN***.)*

What about you?

WOMAN. What about me?

ELLEN. You're female. And young. And white. Why aren't you back on the procreation farm receiving the royal treatment?

DOCTOR. That's really none of your business.

ELLEN. So instead of making babies they send her out into the field to look pretty and do the dirty work?

WOMAN. Are you trying to tell me that I'm pretty or dirty?

ELLEN. Are you a virgin?

(The **WOMAN** *doesn't answer.)*

Do you have ovaries?

WOMAN. Of course I have ovaries.

ELLEN. Nipples? A vagina?

(The **WOMAN** *doesn't answer.)*

There's no number on your neck. Why aren't you wearing a blue bonnet?

DOCTOR. At some point you're going to realize that there are certain things we're simply not going to answer.

ELLEN. How many white infant females have you acquired?

(No answer.)

Give me a number. Under ten? Over a hundred?

WOMAN. Let's just say that if this one passes the examination she'll be part of the first generation.

ELLEN. It sounds like Mrs. Winship is attempting to build a super race.

WOMAN. She's simply trying to embark with the most genetically robust candidates.

ELLEN. Embark.

WOMAN. Yes, embark.

ELLEN. Like some great sea voyage.

WOMAN. Figuratively speaking that's not far off.

ELLEN. Another great ark. It's kind of like the Bible. Or science fiction. Or Hitler. What's Fraulein Winship's background?

WOMAN. Her background is in tremendous, interminable wealth.

ELLEN. American wealth?

WOMAN. Her wealth has no geographical or cultural limits.

ELLEN. Is it from oil?

> *(No answer.)*

Water?

> *(Again, no answer.)*

Diamonds?

> *(Nothing.)*

Espresso beans?

> *(Still nothing.)*

Weapons of mass destruction?

WOMAN. She's a humanist.

ELLEN. A humanist?

WOMAN. That's right.

ELLEN. Define "humanist" for me.

WOMAN. A humanist is a person having a strong interest in or concern for human welfare, values, and dignity.

ELLEN. Yet she also traffics in trading children and doesn't bother showing up for the transaction. What about me?

WOMAN. What about you?

ELLEN. I'm a perfectly healthy woman. You could take me back to the farm with you.

WOMAN. I'm afraid you're a little long in the tooth.

ELLEN. That expression makes me sound like an emaciated she-wolf. I'm barely thirty.

DOCTOR. You're five years too old.

ELLEN. Harsh.

DOCTOR. Mrs. Winship has rigorous standards.

ELLEN. But you could make excellent use of me, good doctor. Look at this skin, these teeth. My ovaries are like fecund fucking frittatas. I'm a registered nurse.

WOMAN. We have an entire medical staff.

DOCTOR. And several highly qualified nurses.

ELLEN. Of course you do.

WOMAN. Besides who would look after him?

> (**ELLEN** *and the* **BOY** *look at each other.*)
>
> (*The keening finally ceases.*)
>
> (*Again, the brief sound of a cold, whistling wind.*)

DOCTOR. We only have a few minutes... Her vitals are good.

WOMAN. Blood type?

DOCTOR. O positive.

WOMAN. The genetics?

DOCTOR. Couldn't be better.

ELLEN. Why didn't you have any trouble getting to this building?

WOMAN. Who said we didn't have trouble? We negotiated your crazy little ladder system.

ELLEN. You're a non-enumerated female. You look like you just stepped off a cruise ship sponsored by Chanel. Are you even perspiring?

WOMAN. It's the Yellow Hour.

ELLEN. The Yellow Hour is a fucking joke. If anything, the Egg Heads use it as a ploy to bait people out of hiding. What's your name? Cindy? Grace? Britney?

WOMAN. My name is of no consequence to you.

ELLEN. I'm entrusting you with an infant child and I'd like to know your name.

WOMAN. You've obviously grown attached to her.

ELLEN. Is it Marsha? Millicent?

WOMAN. It was strongly advised that the child be emotionally unconnected.

ELLEN. I've been caring for her for the past however many months. I'm not a fucking robot.

> *(She pulls the gun on the **WOMAN**, cocks it.)*
>
> *(The **BOY** quickly stands.)*
>
> *(The **DOCTOR** stops examining the baby.)*

Tell me your name.

> *(A brief, intense pause.)*

You think I'm bluffing, look around the room.

DOCTOR. Tell her.

WOMAN. It's Claire.

ELLEN. Claire what?

CLAIRE. Just Claire.

DOCTOR. We don't have last names.

ELLEN. Why not?

CLAIRE. We just don't.

ELLEN. Do you have middle names?

DOCTOR. No.

ELLEN. Where are you from, Claire?

CLAIRE. I'm from Mrs. Winship's farm.

ELLEN. And before that?

CLAIRE. There is no "before that."

ELLEN. You were born and raised there?

CLAIRE. Yes.

ELLEN. Educated, too?

CLAIRE. Yes.

ELLEN. *(Still training the gun on her.)* What exactly do you do for Mrs. Winship, besides trot around the globe collecting genetically acceptable children?

CLAIRE. I don't see why this would matter to you.

ELLEN. It matters because I'm pointing a loaded gun at you. It matters because I'm rarely in the presence of such esteemed fucking well-appointed company and I'm desperate for some conversation.

CLAIRE. I do a great many things.

ELLEN. You're Mrs. Winship's little attaché.

CLAIRE. That's one way of looking at it, although I'm not a dwarf or a six-year-old girl.

ELLEN. Is that the faintest hint of a British accent I'm hearing?

> *(The* **DOCTOR** *produces a gun, sets it to the back of* **ELLEN**'s *head.)*

DOCTOR. Lower the gun.

> *(***ELLEN** *lowers the gun.)*

Set it on the floor.

> *(She does so.)*

Place your hands behind you back.

> *(She does so.)*

> *(The* **DOCTOR** *circles her, retrieves the gun, places it in the small of his back, stands behind* **ELLEN**, *the gun still at the back of her head. He forces her to bend over the tub, head down.)*

Count to five.

ELLEN. *(Terrified.)* One...two...three...four –

> *(The* **DOCTOR** *receives instruction from* **CLAIRE**, *then removes the gun, returns to his business upstage of the typhoid wall.)*

> *(A long silence.)*

> *(The whistling wind.)*

> *(Machine gun fire from the street.)*

CLAIRE. *(To the* **BOY**.) You may sit.

> *(The* **BOY** *sits.)*

> *(The* **DOCTOR** *returns to the infant.)*

ELLEN. *(Clearly shaken.)* Is Mrs. Winship doing business with the Egg Heads?

(**CLAIRE** *says nothing.*)

Did you pay them off to get in here?

(*Again, nothing.*)

Do you even know?

CLAIRE. Mrs. Winship cares deeply about restoring what has been lost. Her main concern is what's possible for the future.

ELLEN. And what does that entail exactly?

CLAIRE. It entails children. Raising them properly. Teaching them good behavior and sound moral principles.

ELLEN. Such as?

CLAIRE. Such as kindness and respect.

ELLEN. And the grave importance of not wearing white after Labor Day?

CLAIRE. (*To the* **DOCTOR**.) Doctor, how are things progressing?

DOCTOR. Almost finished.

ELLEN. How did Mrs. Winship connect with China?

CLAIRE. China the Country?

ELLEN. China, my contact from Third Street.

CLAIRE. I know nothing about China, your contact from Third Street. All I know is a deal was set in place. And now everything has been carried out, as promised. You have what you want and it appears that we do as well. I'm quite sure your so-called Egg Heads will leave you be for a while.

ELLEN. Is that a promise?

CLAIRE. Yes.

ELLEN. Good little errand girl.

CLAIRE. Doctor?

DOCTOR. (*From the kitchen.*) The examination is complete. The infant is acceptable.

> (*He enters the downstage area with an impressive, environmentally protective bio-hazard cape, arranges it over* **CLAIRE** *in a regal manner. This piece also contains a head covering.*)

*(Then the **DOCTOR** crosses upstage of the typhoid wall. As he reaches the threshold of the entryway, a cell phone rings. He pads at his bio-hazard jumpsuit, unzips it, produces a futuristic cell phone, perhaps a simple rectangle of Lucite, begins speaking in fluent Arabic.)*

DOCTOR. *(In Arabic.)* Yes... Yes... Two minutes... The woman and me. We also have a small box... An infant...

(He recites the exact coordinates of their location.)

...We'll be right down.

*(He trains the cell phone on **CLAIRE**, it pulses, taking her photo or some other digital information, puts it away.)*

ELLEN. Why do you have a cell phone? Those don't work anymore.

*(To **CLAIRE**.)* Why does he have a fucking cell phone?

*(The **DOCTOR** removes his white medical jumpsuit, his glasses and shoes. Underneath he is wearing a military uniform, very similar to the one Hakim was wearing, but nicely pressed, very new, with a black ascot. He produces a gas mask, an egg-shaped helmet, puts these on, the gas mask below his beard. He enters the downstage area with a sturdy white box containing the incubator bin and the child. He stands beside **CLAIRE**.)*

CLAIRE. *(To the **BOY**.)* Goodbye, Darius.

DARIUS. Goodbye, ma'am.

CLAIRE. Say goodbye to Doctor Joseph.

DARIUS. Goodbye, Doctor Joseph.

*(The **DOCTOR** crosses to **DARIUS**. **DARIUS** stands. The **DOCTOR** produces Ellen's gun, hands it to him.)*

DOCTOR. Goodbye, Darius.

> *(He rejoins* **CLAIRE** *at the door.)*

CLAIRE. *(To* **ELLEN.***)* I have no doubt that you will be pleased with him. Good luck.

ELLEN. Don't you even want to know my name?

CLAIRE. *(Mid-exit.)* We already know your name.

> *(***CLAIRE** *and the* **DOCTOR** *exit with the infant.)*
>
> *(***ELLEN** *shuts and locks the door.)*
>
> *(Just* **ELLEN** *and* **DARIUS** *now.)*
>
> *(A cold, whistling wind.)*
>
> *(***ELLEN** *crosses to* **DARIUS,** *takes the gun from him, puts it in her waistband, crosses back near the door.)*

DARIUS. May I put my coat on?

ELLEN. Of course.

> *(***DARIUS** *removes his coat from the back of his chair, puts it on, sits.)*

(After a silence.) This must be quite a shock for you.

> *(He says nothing.)*

Did you know you were coming here?

> *(He shakes his head.)*

Are you hungry?

> *(He shakes his head.)*

Thirsty?

> *(He shakes his head.)*

Please talk to me. You have a lovely voice... Did they really know my name?

DARIUS. Yes.

ELLEN. What is it?

DARIUS. Ellen.

ELLEN. What else did they tell you?

DARIUS. Just that I was taking a trip.

ELLEN. This isn't just a trip. You're going to be staying with me.

> (**DARIUS** *simply looks at her.*)

How old are you, Darius?

DARIUS. Fourteen.

> (*Beat.*)

Were you really gonna shoot her?

ELLEN. I don't know. I felt like I could have.

DARIUS. Because she wouldn't tell you her name?

ELLEN. It's strange. You get to a certain point in your life and you really think you know what you're capable of.

> (*The sound of automatic weapons from the street.* **DARIUS** *is clearly uncomfortable.*)

It's very dangerous here, Darius.

> (*He nods.*)

I imagine it was pretty safe at Mrs. Winship's farm.

> (*He nods.*)

Did you ever see soldiers? Or men with guns?

DARIUS. No.

ELLEN. Was there ever violence?

DARIUS. Not really.

> (*The sound of a distant bomb.*)

ELLEN. You must never go outside here. If you go outside you could be killed, do you understand?

DARIUS. Yes ma'am.

> (*It starts to snow through a crack in the skylight.*)

ELLEN. It's snowing in *here* now.
(*Referring to the ceiling.*) At some point we'll have to fix all that.

> (*From the street, a military vehicle slowly rolls by, blaring a famous American pop*

song. Or a cartoon theme song, like the one from Woody Woodpecker.*)*

DARIUS. May I use the toilet?

ELLEN. Of course.

> (**DARIUS** *crosses to it, steps up onto the throne.* **ELLEN** *replaces him at the step stool.*)

Don't flush. It makes too much noise. We only flush when the bombs go off.

> (**DARIUS** *is uncomfortable, attempts to close the shower curtain, but it doesn't work. He steps off the throne, produces a handkerchief, wipes his hands.*)

DARIUS. I'll go later.

> *(He folds the handkerchief, puts it away.)*

ELLEN. So we're going to be spending a lot of time together, Darius. We might get on each other's nerves. I snore. Do you mind snoring?

DARIUS. No.

ELLEN. And I occasionally talk in my sleep.

DARIUS. What do you say?

ELLEN. I don't know. But sometimes it's so loud I wake myself up.

DARIUS. Maybe I could write it down.

ELLEN. Do you know how to write?

DARIUS. A little.

> *(He looks at his hands, a simple, nervous gesture. The snow stops falling.)*

ELLEN. It stopped.

> *(Awkward pause.)*

---

*A license to produce *Through the Yellow Hour* does not include a performance license for any third-party or copyrighted music. Licensees should create an original composition or use music in the public domain. For further information, please see Music Use Note on page 3.

ELLEN. So what did you do at Mrs. Winship's farm?

DARIUS. Worked with the horses mostly.

ELLEN. You fed them?

DARIUS. Fed 'em. Washed 'em. Mucked the stalls.

ELLEN. Did you get to ride them?

DARIUS. Sometimes.

ELLEN. Did you have a favorite horse?

DARIUS. There was this brown mare called Shady.

ELLEN. Do you like horses?

DARIUS. I liked Shady. She could get real nervous, though.

> *(They don't say anything for a moment. He points to the body.)*

Who is that?

ELLEN. Just a man.

DARIUS. Is he dead?

ELLEN. I'm afraid so.

DARIUS. Did you know him?

ELLEN. No.

DARIUS. How long has he been like that?

ELLEN. I honestly couldn't tell you.

DARIUS. Did you kill him?

ELLEN. Yes.

DARIUS. You shot him.

ELLEN. I did. But I thought he was going to hurt me. I had no choice... The men around here are getting castrated and tortured. The threat of getting caught makes them take desperate measures. Do you know what castration means?

DARIUS. On the farm sometimes they do that to the hogs. But they live.

ELLEN. The Egg Heads – those are the bad people – they're not interested in letting anyone live.

DARIUS. Why are they called Egg Heads?

ELLEN. Because they wear these white helmets that look like eggs.

DARIUS. Like the one Doctor Joseph was wearing?

ELLEN. Yes. If you ever see an Egg Head you should hide as fast as possible.

DARIUS. Because they'll castrate me?

ELLEN. I'm afraid so.

DARIUS. There's always a mess of blood when the hogs get done.

> *(The whistling wind.)*
>
> *(**ELLEN** crosses upstage of the typhoid wall, returns with a towel. She wipes the area upstage of the tub where the snow has fallen.)*

ELLEN. There's going to be a lot to clean up around here. I hope you'll help me. Will you?

DARIUS. *(Referring to the dead man.)* Are we gonna bury him?

ELLEN. No, but we can put him in the hallway.

DARIUS. Next to that other man?

ELLEN. Next to him, yes.

DARIUS. When?

ELLEN. Soon. When it's safe.

> *(She crosses downstage left where the space heater has been set. She turns it on, kneels down beside it, warms her hands.)*

DARIUS. Do you have a husband?

ELLEN. He died.

DARIUS. You killed him too?

ELLEN. No.

DARIUS. How'd he die?

ELLEN. He was tortured.

DARIUS. By the Egg Heads?

ELLEN. I'm afraid so.

DARIUS. Aren't you sad?

ELLEN. Very much so, yes.

DARIUS. Why aren't you crying?

ELLEN. I guess you get to a certain point.

DARIUS. And then what?

ELLEN. I don't know how to answer that, Darius. You get too tired maybe. And you forget how.

DARIUS. Are you gonna kill me too?

ELLEN. No. That's the last thing in the world I want to do.

> *(She opens a cupboard, removes a can of peaches, pulls the pop-top.)*

> *(**DARIUS** crosses to the dead man, leans over, studies his face.)*

DARIUS. His eyes are gone.

ELLEN. Does that bother you?

DARIUS. A little.

> *(He looks around. He points to the sleeping nests.)*

That's where we sleep?

> *(**ELLEN** nods.)*

On the floor?

> *(She nods.)*

Does it always smell like this?

ELLEN. Yes, but you'll get used to it.

> *(She offers the peaches, sits on the edge of the bathtub.)*

> *(**DARIUS** crosses to her, takes the peaches, remains standing.)*

You can sit.

> *(He does so. He wraps the can of peaches with his handkerchief, starts to eat them with his fingers.)*

What was Mrs. Winship's farm like?

DARIUS. I'm not supposed to say.

ELLEN. I know you're not supposed to tell me where it is, but what was it like?

DARIUS. There were these big long meadows. And two mountains. One of them had snow on it. And there was a lake.

ELLEN. Was the water clean?

DARIUS. You could swim to the bottom and drink it.

ELLEN. You could drink it right out of the lake?

DARIUS. Like it was from a faucet. You could fish in it, too. I caught bass mostly. Caught some crappie too.

ELLEN. Did anyone get sick there?

DARIUS. Just the animals. This one sheep got worms. When the animals got sick we put apple cider vinegar in their food.

ELLEN. Were there any girls? Besides Claire and Mrs. Winship?

DARIUS. There was this old Mexican lady who made tortillas. And some nurses. And this woman who changed the sheets.

ELLEN. How long have you been there?

DARIUS. Since I was little.

ELLEN. Do you know where you're originally from?

DARIUS. This place called Gary.

ELLEN. Gary, Indiana.

DARIUS. I think so.

ELLEN. Do you remember your parents?

(**DARIUS** *shakes his head.*)

Do you ever think about them? What they might be like?

(*He shakes his head.*)

My husband was from Indiana. Kokomo, Indiana.

DARIUS. Never heard of Kokomo.

ELLEN. It's further south than Gary.

DARIUS. What did he do?

ELLEN. He was a schoolteacher.

DARIUS. Do you miss him?

ELLEN. Very much.

(**DARIUS** *passes the can of peaches to her, wipes his hands with his handkerchief.*)

ELLEN. How many boys were living at the farm?

DARIUS. There were a hundred and seventy-eight of us. I was number forty-one.

ELLEN. And you all worked?

DARIUS. Uh-huh.

ELLEN. With the horses?

DARIUS. Some of them worked with cows. Some with the hogs and the sheep. Some went to school. Before the horses I fed the dogs.

ELLEN. Did you get to go to school too?

DARIUS. No, I just worked.

ELLEN. But others went to school?

DARIUS. Only the white ones.

ELLEN. And the bombs never reached you?

DARIUS. What bombs?

ELLEN. Did you even know what was happening in the rest of the country?

DARIUS. No.

ELLEN. We were attacked. They bombed our major cities and released germs that made people terribly sick. They tortured and killed the men. Very few people have survived.

DARIUS. How come you survived?

ELLEN. Because I'm lucky.

DARIUS. Maybe God picked you.

ELLEN. I'm not sure about God, Darius.

DARIUS. Why not?

ELLEN. It's hard to believe he exists when the world is the way it is.

DARIUS. He exists. He just gets tired.

ELLEN. Who told you that?

DARIUS. Nobody. He gets tired. Like a cow gets tired.

ELLEN. I'm more likely to believe in a cow.

> (*She hands the peaches back to* **DARIUS**.)

DARIUS. When we were coming here there was a bunch of dogs in the street. They weren't like regular dogs. They were eating a man and fighting over his bones.

ELLEN. What were the dogs like at Mrs. Winship's farm?

DARIUS. They were these big white hairy dogs. They only got mean if you messed with the cows or the sheep. Or if you went near their food. Sometimes they would kill a lamb. Then they'd get shot and we'd have to get a new dog.

ELLEN. Well, *this* is what happens when *people* stop being civilized. The people start acting like animals and the animals become savage.

> (**DARIUS** *nods.*)

Seeing all this destruction must be strange for you.

> (**DARIUS** *finishes with the peaches, passes them back.*)

> (**ELLEN** *rises, rinses the can in the bathtub.* **DARIUS** *rises as well, a gentlemanly gesture.*)

You can sit.

> (*She pulls the cigarette from behind her ear.*)

Mind if I smoke?

> (**DARIUS** *shakes his head.*)

> (**ELLEN** *crosses to the stove, lights her cigarette on the burner, smokes, smokes in the doorway of the typhoid wall.*)

DARIUS. That baby was pretty small. Was she yours?

ELLEN. No.

DARIUS. She didn't have a name?

ELLEN. No, but I'm sure she'll get one very soon.

DARIUS. I got traded for her didn't I?

ELLEN. Does that make you angry?

DARIUS. I got traded for a stupid little baby.

ELLEN. Have a lot of boys from the farm been leaving?

DARIUS. This boy Richard had to go away and then they came back with a little girl.

ELLEN. Was she white?

DARIUS. Yes. She had a birthmark on her arm. It had fur growing out of it so they took it off.

ELLEN. Was Richard white?

DARIUS. I think he had some Mexican in him.

ELLEN. Was he your friend?

DARIUS. We used to go swimming and stuff.

ELLEN. Do you miss him?

DARIUS. Yes. He could walk on his hands. He walked all over the place. He was number sixty-eight.

(*He returns the handkerchief to his pocket.*)

That baby's feet were so little.

ELLEN. I'm sure Mrs. Winship will take good care of her. She'll have a nice life.

(*She stubs out her cigarette, preserves it, steps downstage, crosses to the bathtub, stops the drain, starts the water.*)

Have you ever been with a girl, Darius?

DARIUS. No.

ELLEN. Do you like girls?

DARIUS. Yes.

ELLEN. What do you like about them?

DARIUS. They're pretty.

ELLEN. Have you ever thought about making love to a girl?

DARIUS. Yes.

ELLEN. Do you know how to do it?

DARIUS. I think so.

ELLEN. Did someone show you?

DARIUS. I just know. I've seen stuff.

ELLEN. Like what?

DARIUS. How the bull does it to the cows.

ELLEN. I'm going to take my clothes off now so I can get into the bathtub.

>   (**DARIUS** *starts to turn away.*)

You don't have to turn away.

>   (*He turns back, watches her undress. She stands before him, naked.*)

Do you think I'm pretty?

DARIUS. Yes.

>   (**ELLEN** *gets in the bathtub, the water still running.*)

ELLEN. Would you like to get in the tub with me?

DARIUS. I don't know. Maybe.

ELLEN. You can if you want.

DARIUS. It's cold.

ELLEN. It is. It's very cold but the water's warm.

DARIUS. I don't like washing in cold water.

ELLEN. Put your hand in, you can feel it.

>   (**DARIUS** *does so.*)

It's warm, right?

>   (*He nods.*)
>
>   (*The reports of automatic weapons from the street, very close proximity.*)
>
>   (*He removes his hand from the water.*)

DARIUS. What was that?

ELLEN. Guns. But don't be afraid.

DARIUS. Who's shooting them, the Egg Heads?

>   (**ELLEN** *nods.*)

They're the ones with the bombs and the germs?

ELLEN. Yes.

DARIUS. Who are they trying to kill?

ELLEN. I don't know anymore. But we're safe here.

DARIUS. Are you sure?

ELLEN. For now I'm sure, yes.

DARIUS. You promise?

ELLEN. I promise.

DARIUS. Is Doctor Joseph an Egg Head.

ELLEN. I think he's only pretending to be an Egg Head.

DARIUS. Why?

ELLEN. I honestly don't know, Darius.

DARIUS. Should I take my clothes off?

> (**ELLEN** *nods.*)
>
> (**DARIUS** *produces his handkerchief again, spreads it out on the mantle of the fireplace, then removes his buttoned-down shirt, his T-shirt, his trousers, his socks, carefully lies them on the handkerchief. He is in his underwear now.*)

These too?

> (**ELLEN** *nods.*)
>
> (**DARIUS** *removes his underwear. Despite his age, he is mature.*)

ELLEN. Get in.

> (**DARIUS** *joins her in the bathtub.*)

The water feels good, right?

> (*He nods. He settles.* **ELLEN** *stops the water.*)

Take my hand.

> (*He does so. She places it over her heart.*)

Now repeat after me, okay, Darius?

> (*He nods.*)

I'm about to change the world.

> (*He hesitates.*)

Go on, say it.

DARIUS. I'm about to change the world.

ELLEN. The world is going to be a better place.

DARIUS. The world is going to be a better place.

ELLEN. Even in the dark of night, there is always a glimmer.

DARIUS. Even in the dark of night...

ELLEN. ...There is always a glimmer.

DARIUS. What's a glimmer?

ELLEN. It's like a flickering light.

DARIUS. Like a star?

ELLEN. Yes, like a star.

DARIUS. Even in the dark of night there is always a glimmer.

> *(It starts to snow again, though they are both unaware of it now.)*

ELLEN. May I?

> *(**DARIUS** nods.)*

> *(She kisses his forehead, his eyes.)*

Say it again, Darius: The world is going to be a better place.

DARIUS. The world is going to be a better place.

> *(Lights fade as they stare into each other's eyes, hearts open, terrified.)*

> *(Snow falls through the broken ceiling.)*

End of Play